Put Beginning Readers on the Right Track with
ALL ABOARD READING™

The All Aboard Reading series is especially designed for beginning readers. Written by noted authors and illustrated in full color, these are books that children really want to read—books to excite their imagination, expand their interests, make them laugh, and support their feelings. With fiction and nonfiction stories that are high interest and curriculum-related, All Aboard Reading books offer something for every young reader. And with four different reading levels, the All Aboard Reading series lets you choose which books are most appropriate for your children and their growing abilities.

Picture Readers
Picture Readers have super-simple texts, with many nouns appearing as rebus pictures. At the end of each book are 24 flash cards—on one side is a rebus picture; on the other side is the written-out word.

Station Stop 1
Station Stop 1 books are best for children who have just begun to read. Simple words and big type make these early reading experiences more comfortable. Picture clues help children to figure out the words on the page. Lots of repetition throughout the text helps children to predict the next word or phrase—an essential step in developing word recognition.

Station Stop 2
Station Stop 2 books are written specifically for children who are reading with help. Short sentences make it easier for early readers to understand what they are reading. Simple plots and simple dialogue help children with reading comprehension.

Station Stop 3
Station Stop 3 books are perfect for children who are reading alone. With longer text and harder words, these books appeal to children who have mastered basic reading skills. More complex stories captivate children who are ready for more challenging books.

In addition to All Aboard Reading books, look for All Aboard Math Readers™ (fiction stories that teach math concepts children are learning in school) and All Aboard Science Readers™ (nonfiction books that explore the most fascinating science topics in age-appropriate language).

All Aboard for happy reading!

With special thanks to
our editor, Jane O'Connor,
and art director, Ronnie Herman.

Published by Grosset & Dunlap, a division of Penguin Young Readers Group, 345 Hudson
Street, New York, New York 10014. ALL ABOARD READING and GROSSET & DUNLAP
are trademarks of Penguin Group (USA) Inc. Published simultaneously in Canada.
Printed in the U.S.A.

Library of Congress Catalog-in-Publication Data

Dubowski, Cathy East.
    Pirate School / by Cathy East Dubowski ; illustrated by Mark Dubowski.
    p.   cm. – (All aboard reading)
    Summary: At Pirate School, Pete learns to act like a pirate and fight it out, but when he
and a classmate find the treasure at the same time, pirate rules don't seem to work.
        [1. Pirates—Fiction. 2. Schools—Fiction. 3. Treasure hunts—Fiction.] I. Dubowski,
    Mark, ill. II. Title. III. Series.
    PZ7.D8544Pi   1996
    [E]—dc20   95-23241
                                                                                    CIP
                                                                                    AC

ISBN 978-0-448-41132-3   24 25 26 27 28 29 30

Pirate School

By Cathy East Dubowski
and Mark Dubowski

Grosset & Dunlap • New York

Pete's family

was a lot like other families.

Every morning

his mom and dad got breakfast.

His baby sister watched
Jolly Roger's Neighborhood.
And Pete rowed the bus
to school.

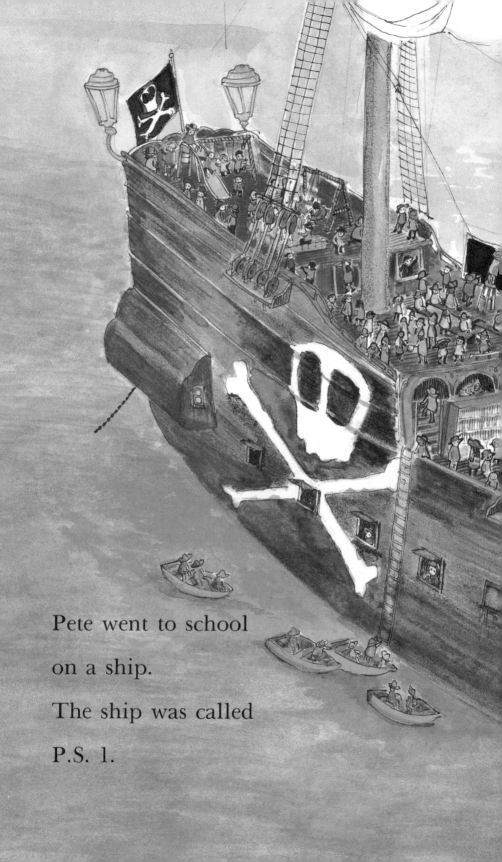

Pete went to school
on a ship.
The ship was called
P.S. 1.

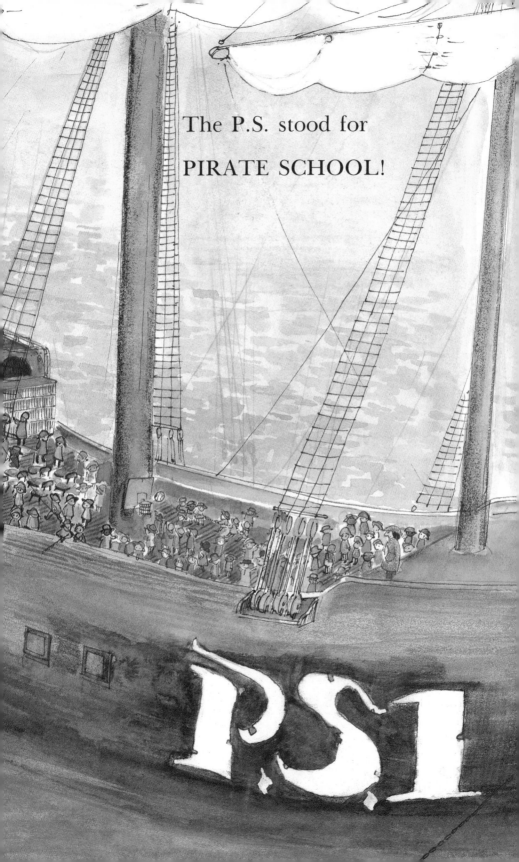

The P.S. stood for

PIRATE SCHOOL!

Pete learned to add

by adding up gold coins.

He learned to subtract
by making classmates
walk the plank!

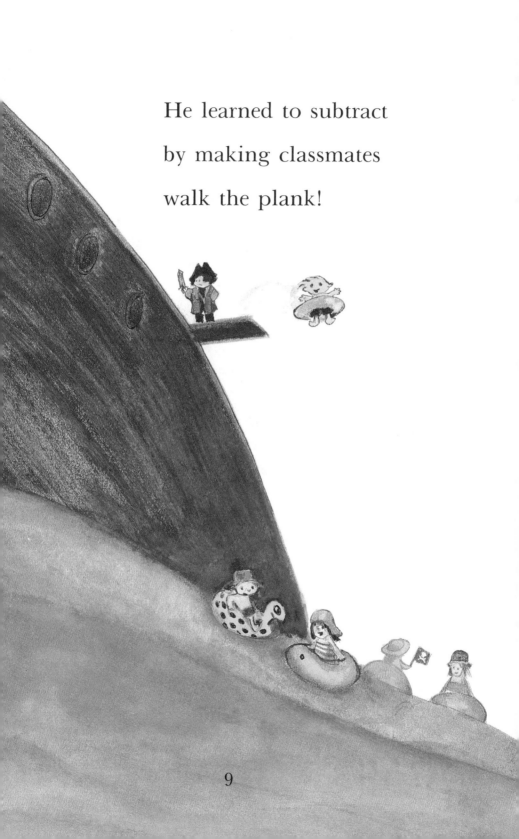

The kids at P.S. 1

were as hard as nails.

And so were the rules.

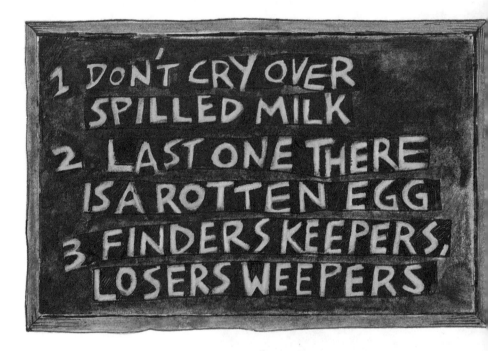

1 DON'T CRY OVER
SPILLED MILK
2. LAST ONE THERE
IS A ROTTEN EGG
3 FINDERS KEEPERS,
LOSERS WEEPERS

Pete liked everything

about Pirate School.

Well, almost everything…

He hated Gregory Grimes the 13th!

(The kids called him Grimy.)

And Grimy hated Pete right back!

"You're too little
to lift the anchor!"
said Grimy.
"You're too big
to get through the hatch!"
said Pete.

"You little shrimp!" shouted Grimy.

"You big whale!" shouted Pete.

"STOP THAT!" yelled their teacher,
Captain Bones.

Captain Bones did not like

kids to call each other names.

"Act like big pirates," he said.

"And <u>fight</u> it out!"

So they did.

Who won?

"I did!" said Grimy.

"No, I did!" said Pete.

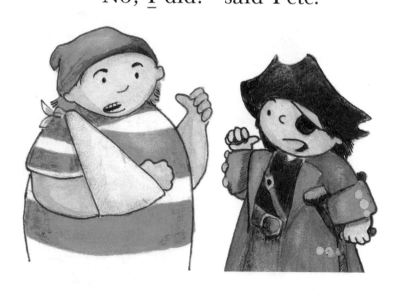

At Pirate School

the biggest day of the year

was Treasure Hunt Day.

Captain Bones held up a map.

"The treasure is hidden here,"

he said.

"X marks the spot.

Find it,

and you get to keep it."

"Finders keepers!" hissed Grimy.

"Losers weepers!" snapped Pete.

All the kids rowed

to the shores of Skull Island.

Pete and Grimy fought all the way.

"I'm going to find

the treasure first!" said Grimy.

"No, I'm going to find it first!"

said Pete.

On Skull Island the class split up.

They all ran off to find

the X that marked the spot.

Pete looked high.

Pete looked low.

"I've got to find that X

before Grimy," he thought.

Pete went deeper and deeper
into the woods.

"That X could be anywhere,"
he said.

So he looked everywhere!

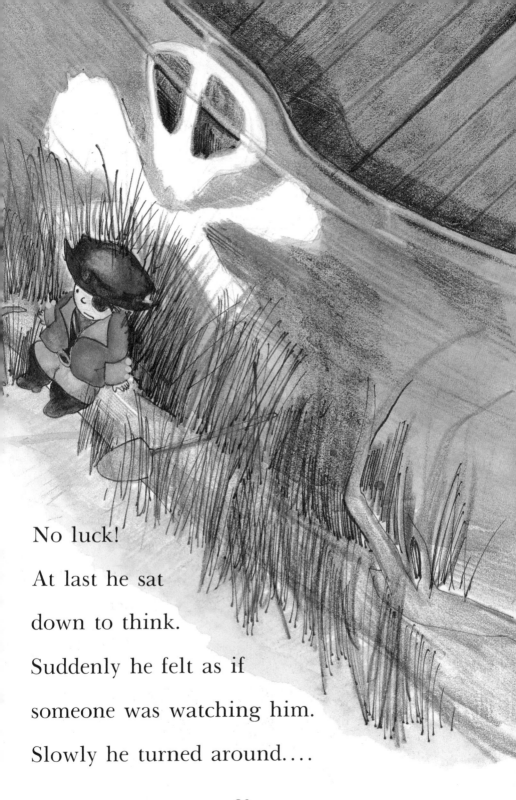

No luck!
At last he sat
down to think.
Suddenly he felt as if
someone was watching him.
Slowly he turned around....

"The X!" he cried.

"I found the X!

It looks just like the one on the map!"

"Forget it!" somebody yelled.

"I found it first!"

It was Grimy!
They had found the X
at the same time!
It was on the side
of an old ship.
"Scram!" said Grimy.
"The treasure is mine!"

"You want to fight about it?"

said Pete.

So they did.

Captain Bones would have been proud.

CRASH!

Pete and Grimy

fell through the rotted deck!

Down, down they went

into the dark!

Pete and Grimy hit bottom.

It was dark and wet and smelly.

Slowly their eyes

got used to the dark.

"L-look!" said Pete.

It was the treasure!

"We found it!" they cheered.

But then they stopped cheering.

They looked around.

There were no steps.

No ladder.

No rope. No door.

They were trapped!

"We'll never get out!"

cried Grimy.

"We'll starve to death.

By the time they find us,

we'll be a pile of bones!"

Pete and Grimy sat down

on the treasure

and waited to die.

"Hey, Pete," said Grimy.

"Are you scared?"

Pete nodded.

"Well, I'm more scared

than you!" said Grimy.

"No, I'm more scared

than you!" said Pete.

But before they could fight it out,

Pete got an idea.

First he got Grimy to help him
turn the treasure chest on its side.
Then he made Grimy
stand on top of the chest.

Then Pete stood on top of Grimy.

"Give me a boost!" Pete cried.

Grimy did.

Pete hit the deck with a thud.

"Ouch!" he said. "I made it!"

He grabbed a rope.

"Tie this to the treasure!"

he called down to Grimy.

Pete turned the crank

and pulled the treasure up.

Pete couldn't wait

to see what was inside.

He opened the chest.

"Wow!" he cried.

He had never seen so much treasure!

"And it's mine!" he shouted.

"All mine!"

"Hey, Pete!" called Grimy.

"What about ME?"

Pete looked down

into the big, dark hole.

Suddenly he had a terrible idea.

"I could just leave him there,"

he thought.

"He'd be a pile of bones.

And I would have all the treasure!"

"Aw, shellfish!" said Pete.

"I just can't do it!

If it weren't for Grimy's help,

I'd still be stuck down there, too."

So he threw down the rope

and pulled Grimy out.

"Thanks, mate," said Grimy.

"I was scared you were

going to leave me."

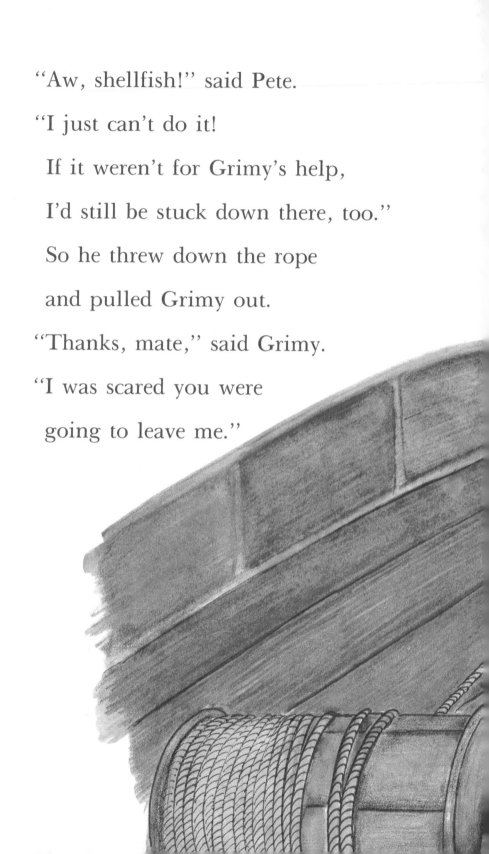

"No, I couldn't do that," said Pete.

"But don't tell Captain Bones

that I saved you.

He'd be mad!"

Together they carried the treasure

back to their boat.

Back at the ship

all the kids cheered.

But Captain Bones frowned.

"We have never had a tie before,"

he said.

"I guess there is only
one thing to do.
Act like big pirates
and fight it out!"

But Pete and Grimy had a better idea.

"We want to split it," said Pete.

"Fifty-fifty," said Grimy.

"Even Steven," said Pete.

So they did.

And that worked out great—

until there was just one coin left.

Pete and Grimy looked at it.

Everyone looked at Pete and Grimy.

What would they do now?

Were they going to fight it out?

No!

They flipped for it!